DEAR OLD DONEGAL

WITHDRAWN

Words and Music by Steve Graham
Pictures by John O'Brien

Clarion Books/New York

Clarion Books
a Houghton Mifflin Company imprint
215 Park Avenue South, New York, NY 10003
Words and Music by Steve Graham
Copyright © 1954 by Leeds Music Corporation
Copyright © renewed
Rights Administered by MCA Music Publishing, A division of MCA INC., 1755 Broadway, New York, NY 10019
International Copyright Secured   All Rights Reserved   Used by Permission
Illustrations copyright © 1996 by John O'Brien

Illustrations executed in pen and ink and watercolor dyes on Strathmore Bristol paper
Text is 19/24-point Cantoria Semibold

Printed in the USA.

Library of Congress Cataloging-in-Publication Data

Graham, Steve.
Dear old Donegal / [words and music] by Steve Graham ; illustrated by John O'Brien.
p.   cm.
Summary: Through the rhyming verses of this song an Irish immigrant to the United States relates his success
in his new country and his delight at the prospect of going back to Ireland.
ISBN 0-395-68187-1
1. Children's songs—Texts.   [1. Ireland—Songs and music.   2. Songs.]   I. O'Brien, John, 1953– ill.   II. Title.
PZ8.3.G729De   1996
782.42164'0268—dc20
[E]   95-21778
CIP
AC
WOZ 10 9 8 7 6 5 4 3 2 1

For Tessie and the O'Briens,
and Patrick and the McGuigans.
—J.O'B.

It seems like only yesterday
I sailed from out of Cork,

A wanderer from Erin's isle

I landed in New York.

There wasn't a soul to greet me there,
A stranger on your shore,

But Irish luck was with me here
And riches came galore.

And now that I'm goin' back again
To dear old Erin's isle,
My friends will meet me on the pier
And greet me with a smile.

Their faces, sure, I've almost forgot—
I've been so long away—
But me mother will introduce them all
And this to me will say:

Shake hands with your Uncle Mike, me boy,
And here is your sister Kate,

And there's the girl you used to swing
Down by the garden gate.

Shake hands with all of the neighbors
And kiss the colleens all—

You're as welcome as the flow'rs in May
To dear old Donegal.

They'll give a party when I go home.
They'll come from near and far,

They'll line the roads for miles and miles
With Irish jauntin' cars.

The spirits'll flow and we'll be gay,
We'll fill your hearts with joy,

The piper'll play an Irish reel
To greet the Yankee boy.

We'll dance and sing the whole night long,
Such fun as never seen—
The lads'll be decked in corduroy,
The colleens wearin' green,

There'll be thousands there that I never saw—
I've been so long away—
But me mother will introduce them all
And this to me will say:

Meet Branigan,

Fannigan,

Milligan, Gilligan,

Duffy, McCuffy,

Malachy, Mahone,

Rafferty, Lafferty,
Donnelly, Connelly,

Dooley, O'Hooley,
Muldowney, Malone,

Madigan, Cadigan,
Lanihan, Flanihan,
Fagan, O'Hagan,
O'Hoolihan, Flynn,

Shanihan, Manihan,
Fogarty, Hogarty,
Kelly, O'Kelly,
McGuinness, McGuinn.

Shake hands with your Uncle Mike, me boy,
And here is your sister Kate,
And there's the girl you used to swing
Down by the garden gate.

Shake hands with all of the neighbors
And kiss the colleens all—
You're as welcome as the flow'rs in May
To dear old Donegal!

AFTERWORD

Between 1820 and 1975, about 47 million people came to the United States from other countries. About one in ten was Irish. In the nineteenth century, opportunities in Ireland were limited, especially for Catholics; many Irish people came to America to escape lives of dire poverty.

Most Irish immigrants settled in cities like Boston and New York and took jobs in construction and in domestic service. Others worked building canals and railroads. Although for most of the Irish immigrants life in America wasn't as hard as it would have been in Ireland, the Irish faced hardships here as well.

By the 1940s, when "Dear Old Donegal" was written, popular culture had adopted a sentimental notion of Ireland and the Irish that had great entertainment value. Films like *The Quiet Man* (1952) depicted a picturesque rural community filled with quaint country folk. The story told in "Dear Old Donegal" is an idealized version of the immigrant experience, playing on the popular idea of the Irish as emotional people who have large, close families and love a good party. With its lilting melody in 6/8 time, the song is meant to sound like a traditional Irish jig.

Nothing is known about composer/lyricist Steve Graham, other than that the name may have been a pseudonym for a song writer named Michael H. Goldsen (1912-1980?). "Dear Old Donegal" was popularized by movie and radio star Bing Crosby, a singer renowned for his easy, romantic vocal style, called crooning. Crosby played an Irish priest in *The Bells of Saint Mary's* and in *Going My Way*, for which he won an Oscar.

My father's father was among the millions who came to this country from Ireland—from Strabane, a town not far from Donegal. My father's mother's family came from Cork. I saw picture book possibilities in "Dear Old Donegal" after finding the sheet music in my (Italian) mother's piano bench.

—John O'Brien

DEAR OLD DONEGAL

by Steve Graham

Arranged by Paul Alan Levi

Verse

It seems like on- ly yes- ter- day I sailed from out of Cork,___ A
They'll give a par- ty when I go home. They'll come from near and far;___ They'll

wan- der- er from Er- in's isle I land- ed in New York.___ There was- n't a soul___ to
line the roads for miles and miles With I- rish jaun- tin' cars. The spir- its- 'll flow___ and

greet me there, A stran- ger on your shore,___ But I- rish luck was with me here And
we'll be gay, We'll fill your hearts with joy,___ The pip- er'll play an I- rish reel to

rich- es came ga- lore.___ And now that I'm go- in' back a- gain To dear old Er- in's
greet the Yan- kee boy.___ We'll dance and sing the whole night long, Such fun as nev- er

isle,___ My friends will meet me on the pier And greet me with a smile.___ Their
seen—___ The lads- 'll be decked in cord- u- roy, The col- leens wear- in' green,___ There'll

fa- ces, sure, I've al- most for- got— I've been so long a- way— But me mo- ther will in- tro-
be thou- sands there that I nev- er saw— I've been so long a- way— But me mo- ther will in- tro-